Pokémon

Get Well, Pikachu!

Adapted by Tracey West

OFFICIAL
Pokémon
EXPERT'S
CLUB

SCHOLASTIC INC.
New York Toronto London Auckland Sydney
Mexico City New Delhi Hong Kong Buenos Aires

Published by Scholastic Inc.
90 Old Sherman Turnpike, Danbury, CT 06816.

SCHOLASTIC and associated logos are trademarks and/or registered trademarks of Scholastic Inc.

ISBN-13: 978-0-439-72153-0
ISBN-10: 0-439-72153-9

First Scholastic Printing, November 2004

Ash and Pikachu were on their way to a new land.

But something was wrong with the little yellow Pokémon.

When their ship landed, Ash ran to a video phone. He called Professor Birch, a friend of Professor Oak's.

Professor Birch's assistant answered. "Your Pikachu looks terrible!" he said. "Professor Birch will be right there."

Minutes later, Professor Birch came speeding up in his car.

"You must be Ash," he said. "Hop in! We need to get Pikachu to my lab right away!"

"Is Pikachu going to be okay?"
Ash asked.

"I don't know," Professor Birch
said. "Pikachu has too much
electricity. And it can't get rid
of it. That can happen to Electric
Type Pokémon."

Soon they reached the professor's lab. Professor Birch strapped Pikachu to a strange machine.

"This will get rid of Pikachu's trapped electricity," he said.

But
Pikachu
still had
too much
electricity!

Boom!
The machine
exploded. It blasted a hole in the wall.

Pikachu felt sick and confused. It ran out of the lab.

"Pikachu!" Ash yelled. "Come back!"

Then Ash ran after his Pokémon.

Professor Birch caught up to Ash. They decided to split up and look for Pikachu.

"But be careful," Professor Birch said. "Pikachu has way too much electricity. Pikachu could explode!"

Professor Birch ran as fast as he could.

Then he tripped! He fell down a hill.

Thump!

He landed right on top of a
Poochyena!

"Sorry," said Professor Birch. "I did not mean to drop in on you like that."

But the Pokémon did not understand the professor's joke. It growled and snarled. Then more Poochyena came.

Professor Birch climbed up a tree.

"Don't be angry, Poochyena," he said.

Then he saw a girl on top of the hill.

"May!" he called. "Help me!"

Professor Birch had dropped his bag on the grass.

"Take a Poké Ball from my bag and throw it," he told May.

"But I have never thrown a Poké Ball before," May said.

May threw the Poké Ball, and out came a Mudkip!

"Mudkip, use Water Gun!" May yelled.

The Water Pokémon let loose with a Water Gun attack—right in May's face!

Crack! Professor Birch fell from the tree. He had to do something fast.

"Mudkip!" he yelled. Mudkip raced down the hill. "Use Water Gun on the Poochyena!"

Mudkip squirted the Poochyena. All the Poochyena ran away.

Nearby, Ash
found Pikachu.
"Don't
move, Pikachu!"
Ash said.

But Pikachu was so sick, it did
not know who Ash was.
Zap! Pikachu gave Ash a shock.

Professor Birch and May ran up to Ash and Pikachu.

"Ash, get away from Pikachu," the professor said. "Pikachu could explode!"

Pikachu wiggled out of Ash's arms. It ran away . . . and fell off of a cliff!

"No!" Ash yelled. He dove after his friend.

Ash grabbed Pikachu in one
hand. He grabbed onto a tree
branch with his other hand.
    "Hang on," Ash told Pikachu.

Professor Birch and May threw down a rope.

Ash tried to climb. But Pikachu could not control his electricity.

Zap! Zap! Zap! Pikachu shocked Ash again and again.

Ash did not give up. He carried Pikachu to the top of the cliff.

"We should get Pikachu back to the lab," said Professor Birch.

But then Ash heard a voice.

"Prepare for trouble!" said the voice.

"It's Team Rocket!" Ash cried.
Jessie, James, and Meowth
were trying to steal Pokémon again.
This time, they rode in a giant
red robot!

"This robot will beat that pesky Pikachu at its own game!" Meowth bragged.

The robot's hand came down
and grabbed Pikachu.

"Pikaaaaaa!" Pikachu tried to
shock the robot.

"Ha-ha!" said Meowth. "Pikachu
can't hurt this robot. It will absorb
all of Pikachu's electricity!"

"Pikaaaaa!" Pikachu did not give up.

Lots and lots of electricity came out of Pikachu.

The robot could not absorb it all.

Boom! The robot exploded.

"We are blasting off again!" Team Rocket cried.

Ash and his new friends rushed
Pikachu back to the lab.
"Pikachu will be fine after a good
night's sleep," said Professor Birch.
Ash stayed with Pikachu all night.

In the morning, Pikachu sat up and smiled.

"Hooray!" Ash cried. "Pikachu is all better!"

Outside, Ash and Pikachu saw
May. She had a little Pokémon
with her.

"This is Torchic, a Fire Pokémon,"
May said. "Torchic is my first
Pokémon ever!"

Pikachu and Torchic started to
run and play.

Ash smiled.

"I am happy that you are better, Pikachu," Ash said. "And I am also happy that we made some new friends!"

"Pika, pika!" Pikachu agreed.

Who's That Electric Pokémon?

37

See page 45 for the answer.

Electric Ears

Can you tell who these Electric Pokémon are by just looking at their ears?

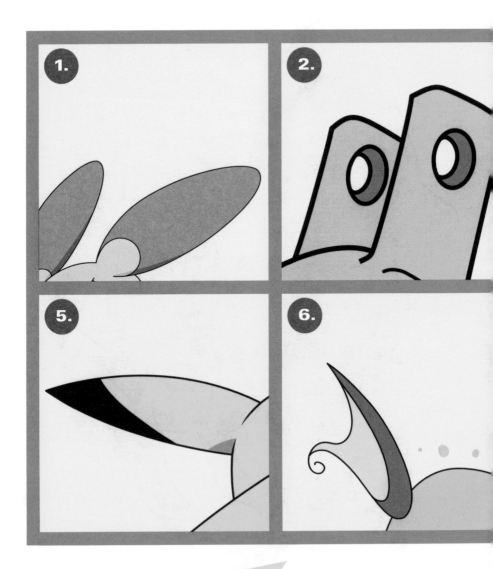

Check page 45 or your *Electric Pokédex* for the answers.

Battle Time!

Now it is your turn to battle! Read about each battle below. Then pick the best Pokémon to use against your opponent. In each battle, all of the Pokémon are the same level.

1. Awww. Your opponent starts with a cute Pikachu! But Pikachu has powerful Electric attacks. Which Pokémon should you choose to battle it?

Sandshrew™	Surskit™	Hoothoot™
(Ground)	(Bug/Water)	(Normal/Flying)

2. Watch out! Your opponent's Treecko looks tough. Which Pokémon should go against this Grass Pokémon?

Electrike™
(Electric)

Combusken™
(Fire/Fighting)

Staryu™
(Water)

3. Look! Up in the sky! It's Taillow, a Normal/Flying Pokémon. Which one of these Pokémon will beat it?

Grovyle™
(Grass)

Registeel™
(Steel)

Mareep™
(Electric)

41

Check page 45 or your *Pokédex* books for the answers.

Which Pokémon Doesn't Belong?

Two of the Pokémon in each row are the same type. One is not. Can you guess which one does not belong?

1. Pikachu™   Electrike™   Arcanine™

2. Torchic™   Wingull™   Magby™

3. Poochyena™   Zigzagoon™   Absol™

4.

Mudkip™   Electrode™   Pichu™

5.

Meowth™   Aipom™   Wynaut™

6.

Grovyle™   Bellossom™   Kirlia™

7.

Magikarp™   Bulbasaur™   Wailmer™

43

Check page 45 or your *Ultimate Sticker Book* for the answers.

Electric Pokémon Jokes

What's Pikachu's favorite dance?

The Electric Slide

What did the Pichu say to Pikachu?

I love you watts and watts!

How did the first person to discover Electric Pokémon feel?

Shocked!

What's cuter than one Pichu?

Two Pichu

Why is Zapdos so dangerous?

Because it doesn't know how to conduct itself!

Knock knock!
Who's there?
Raichu!
Raichu who?
Bless you! Do you need a tissue?

Answers

Page 37: Who's That Electric Pokémon?

Manectric!

Pages 38–39: Electric Ears

1. Minun
2. Elekid
3. Plusle
4. Ampharos

5. Pikachu
6. Raichu
7. Pichu
8. Mareep

Pages 40–41: Battle Time!

1. Sandshrew (Ground beats Electric)
2. Combusken (Fire beats Grass)
3. Mareep (Electric beats Normal/Flying)

Pages 42–43: Which Pokémon Doesn't Belong?

1. Arcanine (Fire)
2. Wingull (Water/Flying)
3. Zigzagoon (Normal)
4. Mudkip (Water)

5. Wynaut (Psychic)
6. Kirlia (Psychic)
7. Bulbasaur (Grass)